This book belongs to:

Contents

Ladybird

Cover illustration by Paula Martyr
Text pages 31–32 by Judith Nicholls (© MCMXCVII)

A catalogue record for this book is available
from the British Library

Published by Ladybird Books Ltd
A subsidiary of the Penguin Group
A Pearson Company

© LADYBIRD BOOKS LTD MCMXCVII

LADYBIRD and the device of a Ladybird are trademarks of
Ladybird Books Ltd Loughborough Leicestershire UK

Monster haircut!

written by Marie Birkinshaw
illustrated by Paula Martyr

Mum looked at Gemma.
"Your hair's too long,"
Mum said. "It's time you
went to the hairdressers'."

"Oh, no," said Gemma.

"Oh, yes," said Mum.
"I'll call Sandra to see if
she can do it."

Gemma pulled a face.

"Oh, Mum! Can't we go somewhere new? somewhere new? Sandra's so boring," she said.

So Mum took Gemma
to the new hairdressers'
in town.

Gemma sat down.
A weird hairdresser put
a gown round her neck.

Gemma pulled a face.

"Would Madam like green hair?" the hairdresser asked.

Just then another hairdresser came running over. "Oh, no!" he said.

"Green wouldn't be right at all. I think pink and yellow would look much better."

Gemma pulled a face.

"Who wants to look like that?" she said. "Come on, Mum! Let's go to Sandra's."

The hairdressers pulled faces at one another!

"Oh, no! Don't go to Sandra's," they said. "She's so boring!"

Who am I?

written by Shirley Jackson
illustrated by Allan Wittert

My first is in wall,
but it isn't in ball.

My second is in dog,
but it isn't in dig.

My third is in bear,
but it isn't in bean.

My fourth is in mouse,
but it isn't in house.

Who am I?

Worm!

Looking for gold

written by Marie Birkinshaw
illustrated by Pauline King

Dad was in the garden.
I was helping him
to put up a fence.

Dad asked, "Do you think we'll find some gold in this hole?"

I said, "I don't know. Let's have a look!"

In went the spade.

We found

a spider,

a beetle,

lots of worms

and some soil.

In went the spade again.
This time we found

a bird's feather,

some little pebbles,

a snail's shell

and more soil.

The spade went in again, and we found some black rock, an old broken pot and lots more soil!

I was getting bored.
"Isn't that hole big enough?"
I asked.

"Just one more spadeful,"
said Dad.

Then his spade hit…

GOLD!

Soil Facts

- Soil is the loose covering of broken rocks and decaying material that covers the rock around the Earth's surface.

- Some of the creatures that live in the soil are called *decomposers*. These include worms, bacteria, fungi and algae. They eat the remains of dead plants and animals, and help to improve the soil.

- A teaspoonful of soil may contain billions of different bacteria.

- About 10 tonnes of soil can pass through the average worm each year. The waste soil is sometimes passed to the surface as worm casts. This can raise the surface of the soil by about 15–20cms every 100 years. Worm burrows help to break up the soil, allowing in air and water.

Soil settles into different levels. Each level contains particular things that make up soil.

Leaf litter and other decaying plants and animals.

Topsoil – a dark and fertile layer of soil where most of the decomposers live.

Subsoil – richer, older soil where deep tree roots grow.

Weathered rock – broken pieces of bedrock.

Bedrock – solid rock at the Earth's surface.

The spider's walk

written by Judith Nicholls
illustrated by David Mostyn

There's a big, hairy spider,
Climbing the door.

Here's a big, hairy spider,
Back on the floor.

There's a big, hairy spider,
Creeping to you.
Nearer and nearer,
  nearer and nearer.
Here's a big, hairy spider…
What will you do?

RUN!

The spider's walk

Help your child with any words he cannot read, and then have fun reading this rhyme faster and faster – with dramatic actions.

New words

Encourage your child to use some of these new words to help him to write his own very simple stories and rhymes. Go back to look at earlier books and their wordlists to practise other words. The Soil Facts are for you to share with your child to motivate him to find out more. Vocabulary used is not included in the list of new words.

is specially designed to help your child learn to read. It will complement all the methods used in schools.

Parents took part in extensive research to ensure that **Read with Ladybird** would help your child to:

- take the first steps in reading
- improve early reading progress
- gain confidence in new-found abilities.

The research highlighted that the most important qualities in helping children to read were that:

- books should be fun – children have enough 'hard work' at school
- books should be colourful and exciting
- stories should be up to date and about everyday experiences
- repetition and rhyme are especially important in boosting a child's reading ability.

The stories and rhymes introduce the 100 words most frequently used in reading and writing.

These 100 key words actually make up half the words we use in speech and reading.

The three levels of **Read with Ladybird** consist of 22 books, taking your child from two words per page to 600-word stories.

Read with Ladybird will help your child to master the basic reading skills so vital in everyday life.

Ladybird have successfully published reading schemes and programmes for the last 50 years. Using this experience and the latest research, **Read with Ladybird** has been produced to give all children the head start they deserve.